PUFFIN BOOKS
Published by the Penguin Group: London, New York, Australia,
Canada, India, Ireland, New Zealand and South Africa
Penguin Books Ltd, Registered Offices: 80 Strand, London WC2R 0RL, England

puffinbooks.com

First published by Abelard-Schuman Ltd 1982
Published in Puffin 1984
Reissued in this format 2008

072

ISBN: 978–0–140–50446–0

Dear Zoo

Rod Campbell

PUFFIN

I wrote to the zoo
to send me a pet.
They sent me an ...

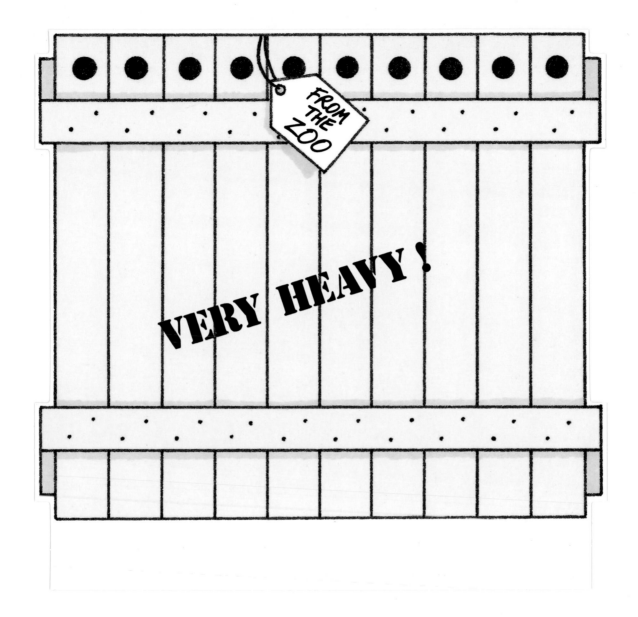

He was too big!
I sent him back.

So they sent me a ...

He was too tall!
I sent him back.

So they sent me a ...

He was too fierce!
I sent him back.

So they sent me a ...

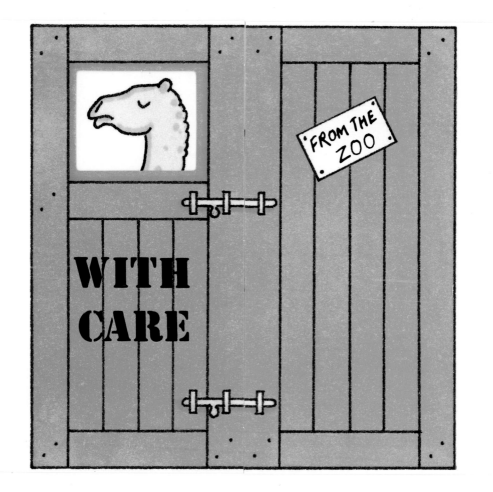

He was too grumpy!
I sent him back.

So they sent me a ...

He was too scary!
I sent him back.

So they sent me a ...

He was too naughty!
I sent him back.

So they sent me a ...

He was too jumpy!
I sent him back.

So they thought
very hard, and
sent me a ...

He was perfect!
I kept him.